Stella
the Star
Fairy

For Molly and Lizzie Barratt
two special fairy fans

Special thanks to
Narinder Dhami

ISBN-10: 0-545-06776-6
ISBN-13: 978-0-545-06776-8

All rights reserved. Published by Scholastic Inc., 557 Broadway, New
York, NY 10012, by arrangement with Rainbow Magic Limited.

SCHOLASTIC, LITTLE APPLE, and associated logos are
trademarks and/or registered trademarks of Scholastic Inc.
RAINBOW MAGIC is a trademark of Rainbow Magic Limited.
Reg. U.S. Patent & Trademark Office and other countries.

12 11 10 9 8 7 6 5 4 3 2 1   8 9 10 11 12 13/0
Printed in the U.S.A.

First Scholastic printing, September 2008

Stella
the Star
Fairy

by Daisy Meadows

SCHOLASTIC INC.

New York   Toronto   London   Auckland   Sydney
Mexico City   New Delhi   Hong Kong   Buenos Aires

The
Fairyland
Palace

The Fairyland Christmas Tree

Wetherbury Village

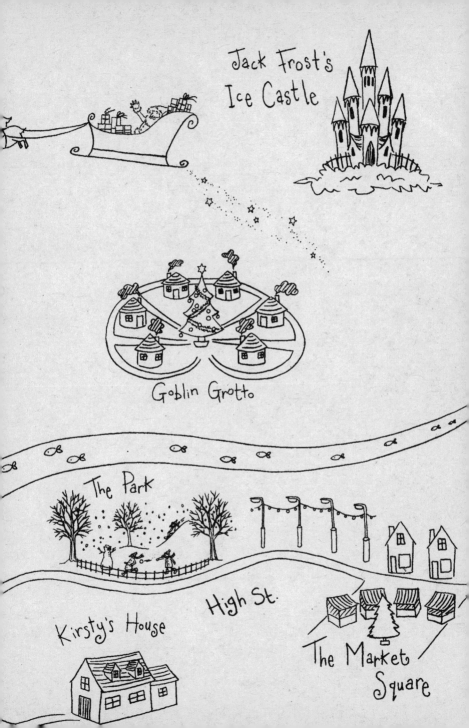

Jack Frost's
Ice Castle

Goblin Grotto

The Park

High St.

Kirsty's House

The Market
Square

The Magical
Missing Candle

Christmas mischief I have planned,
So, goblins, go to Fairyland!
Find the fairy Christmas tree
Bearing magic items — three.

Steal these special decorations
To spoil Christmas celebrations.
Candle, glass ball, magic star —
Take them where no fairies are!

**Find the hidden letters in the stars
throughout this book. Unscramble all
7 letters to make a special holiday word!**

Contents

Darkness Falls

Mrs. Tate popped her head around the door. "Are you ready, girls?" she asked. "It's time to leave for the Christmas Fair."

"Coming, Mom," Kirsty said, jumping up.

"I'm really glad I could come and visit," said Rachel Walker, as she followed her best friend into the hall to get their coats. Rachel was visiting over Christmas break. Her parents were picking her up on Christmas Eve.

"Me, too," Kirsty replied. "You're going to love the fair. And who knows . . . we might even see a Christmas fairy!"

Rachel and Kirsty thought they were the luckiest girls in the world, because they had become friends with the fairies! Whenever the fairies were in trouble, they asked the girls for help. Usually cold Jack Frost was causing magical mayhem with the help of his nasty goblins.

"I forgot to tell you!" Kirsty said, pulling on her boots. "Every year, someone from my school is chosen to be the fair's Christmas King or Queen. This year, it's my friend Molly."

"Wow! I bet she's really excited," said Rachel, smiling. "I'd love to be the Christmas Queen!"

Kirsty nodded as her parents joined them.

"Everybody ready?" Mrs. Tate said. "Then let's go!"

"Did someone turn off the Christmas tree lights?" Mr. Tate asked. "They were on a few minutes ago, but now they're not."

Everyone shook their heads. Kirsty peeked into the living room, where the tree stood.

"The switch is still on," she pointed out.

"The lights must be broken," Mr. Tate decided. "Never mind, I'll fix them when we get back."

"Yes, it's time to go," Kirsty's mom agreed. "The parade starts soon!"

Quickly, they all left the house and walked up Twisty Lane toward High Street and Wetherbury Market Square.

"I can hear music," Rachel said, clapping her hands excitedly.

Even though it was a cold, frosty night, the square was packed with people! They bustled around stalls selling brightly-painted tree decorations, Christmas cookies, hot chocolate, and gifts. There was even a merry tune playing on an old organ.

"Isn't it great?" Kirsty said, her eyes shining. She pointed at a raised platform in the middle of the square. The mayor of Wetherbury was standing there next to a large switch. "It'll be even better when the Christmas Queen turns on the lights," Kirsty added.

Rachel glanced around. She could see dark shapes made out of unlit lightbulbs above their heads, but it was hard to figure out what the shapes were. She was looking forward to seeing them all lit up.

"Ooh, I can't wait to see Molly!" Kirsty exclaimed, as the parade began.

The first float that rumbled into the square was decorated like Santa's workshop. Elves were making toys, and Santa sat on a golden sleigh!

"Oh, look!" Rachel gasped, as another float came into view. It carried a huge dollop of papier-mâché fruitcake with a sprig of holly on top. More floats followed, all looking colorful and Christmassy!

"Here's Molly," Kirsty said to Rachel as the final float appeared. "Doesn't she look pretty?"

Kirsty's friend was dressed in white and silver. Her dress had a long full skirt, scattered here and there with sparkling snowflakes. She wore a glittering silver tiara on her head and sat on a jeweled throne, waving at the crowd. Behind her was an ice palace, decorated with gleaming icicles.

Rachel nudged Kirsty. "The Christmas Queen's palace is much prettier than Jack Frost's gloomy ice castle!" she whispered. Kirsty nodded eagerly.

The float stopped next to the platform. The mayor helped Molly up the steps as the crowd clapped.

"I would like to wish everyone in Wetherbury a very merry Christmas!" Molly announced. Then she pulled the light switch with a flourish.

The square lit up in a blaze of
color as the lightbulbs sprang
to life. Everyone *oohed*
and *aahed* as they
gazed around.
"This is amazing!"
Kirsty breathed.
"It's beautiful,"
Rachel
agreed.
There were
hundreds of
snowflakes in
different sizes
strung on wires
overhead, and they
all glittered with
rainbow-colored lights.

The Christmas Queen had come down from the platform now and was waving at the two girls.

"Hi, there!" Molly called, her face glowing with excitement. "Did you like my float?"

"It was beautiful!" Kirsty replied. "Molly, this is my friend Rachel."

"Hi, Molly," said Rachel, admiring Molly's sparkling dress. "You look so pretty!"

"And these are definitely the best lights Wetherbury has ever had!" Kirsty added.

But just then, one of the snowflakes above their heads began to flicker. As the girls glanced upward, every single one of the beautiful snowflake lights suddenly went out!

Trouble in Fairyland

Everyone gasped, including the girls.

"What happened?" asked Kirsty. "The lights were fine a minute ago."

The mayor climbed onto the platform and called for everyone's attention. "Please don't worry," he said firmly. "We'll have the lights fixed soon. And in the meantime, enjoy the fair!"

"It's too bad about the lights," Molly said. "But I've had a great night so far, anyway!"

"I'm sure the lights will be fixed by tomorrow," Kirsty replied.

"I hope so," Molly agreed. Then she smiled at the girls. "Now, I have to go and hand out presents to the children who rode on the floats."

"A Christmas Queen's work is never done!" Kirsty said with a grin. Molly laughed and waved as she walked away. Rachel and Kirsty headed back to find Mr. and Mrs. Tate.

"What a pity that the lights went out," said Kirsty's mom. "They looked so pretty."

"I'm glad I only have to fix *our* tree lights and not all these bulbs!" said Mr. Tate, smiling and shaking his head. "Let's go home and get warm."

As Mr. and Mrs. Tate walked on ahead, Kirsty turned to Rachel. "It's awfully dark tonight. There isn't a single star in the sky —" Suddenly she stopped dead, clutching her friend's arm. "Rachel, look!"

Rachel stared ahead. High Street was lined with

lampposts decorated with more of the snowflake lights. The one closest to the girls had a couple of lightbulbs that were shining brightly!

Kirsty looked puzzled. "How can those bulbs be on, when all the others aren't working?" she asked.

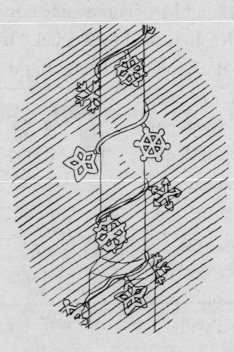

But Rachel didn't reply. Was she imagining it, or had she just seen a swirl of glitter that looked like . . . fairy magic?

"Rachel! Kirsty!" called a tiny, musical voice.

"It's a fairy!" Rachel gasped.

The fairy who was fluttering toward them, blond ponytail bobbing, was dressed in Christmas green and red. A string of sparkly gold Christmas lights was looped around the waist of her little red dress. She wore a green feather boa around her neck.

"Hello!" Kirsty said breathlessly as the fairy landed lightly on her shoulder. "What's your name?"

"I'm Stella the Star Fairy," the fairy explained. "I'm in charge of all the sparkly Christmas decorations, the lights on Christmas trees, and the stars that guide Santa and his reindeer on Christmas night!"

"Were you trying to turn the bulbs back on?" asked Rachel.

Stella's delicate wings drooped as she hung her head. "I was," she sighed. "But look!"

The girls glanced up at the lamppost.

The bulbs that Stella had turned on had gone out again!

"That's what happens every single time," Stella said glumly. "I turn a bulb on, but it just goes out again!"

"Don't worry, Stella," said Kirsty. "They'll be fixed soon."

But Stella shook her head. "No, you don't understand, Kirsty," she replied. "This is all Jack Frost's fault!"

"Jack Frost?" Kirsty repeated, glancing at Rachel. "Is he trying to ruin Christmas again?"

"Yes." Stella sighed. "Every year at Christmastime, we have a huge Christmas tree in Fairyland. There are three very special and magical ornaments on it. But this year, wicked Jack Frost sent his goblins to steal them. Now they're gone!"

"Oh no!" Kirsty said. "Why are these ornaments so special?"

"The first one is the shining white candle," replied Stella. "It controls all the Christmas decorations in the human world."

"So that's why the Wetherbury snowflakes went out!" Rachel exclaimed.

Stella nodded. "The second is
the glass ball. That
controls all the
Christmas tree
lights," she
went on.

"Our tree
lights!" Kirsty
gasped. "That's
why they're not
working."

"And the third is the shining star from
the top of the tree," Stella continued.
"The star makes sure that the real stars
shine in the night sky, to guide Santa
when he's delivering presents. We have
to get all three of the ornaments back
from the goblins, or Christmas will
be ruined!"

"Do you know where the magical ornaments are?" Kirsty asked.

"Well, when we realized what the goblins were doing, we chased them," explained Stella. "Only the goblin with the magic star made it back to Goblin Grotto. The others were forced to escape into the human world. They took the magic candle and glass ball with them!"

"Can we help find them?" asked Rachel.

Stella beamed at her. "I was hoping you'd say that!" she declared. "The candle and the glass ball became larger when they entered the

human world, so they're big enough for you to spot."

"Then we'll look for them," said Rachel, determined. "We won't let Jack Frost ruin Christmas!"

"Thank you, girls!" cried Stella happily. "I'll rush back to Fairyland and tell the king and queen that you're helping me. But remember not to search too hard — the fairy magic will come to you!" And with a wave of her glittering wand, Stella flew away into the night.

Carols and Candles

"There isn't much time before Christmas," Rachel remarked, as she finished her cereal the following morning. "I hope we can get the candle, the glass ball, and the star back by then."

"We'll do our best," Kirsty replied. "Mom says we can go Christmas shopping in Wetherbury later, so we should keep our eyes open for fairy magic!"

After lunch, the girls bundled up and headed into town. Mr. Tate stayed behind, struggling to fix the Christmas tree lights. Even though the sun was shining in the pale blue sky, there was a frosty chill in the air.

"Maybe we'll have some snow tonight," Kirsty said eagerly.

"Look," Rachel said, nudging her friend. "The electricians are trying to fix the snowflake lights."

Two men on top of long ladders tinkered with the bulbs, as shoppers milled around on the street below.

"They won't have much luck unless we get the magic candle back," Kirsty whispered.

The square was full of market stalls and busy stores. The floats and the platform from the night before were gone. A tall Christmas tree had been set up in their place! It was decorated with shiny glass balls, tinsel, and lights, though they weren't working. A small group of children was gathered on one side of the tree, holding candles in silver holders and singing carols.

"Doesn't that sound Christmassy?"
Kirsty said with a grin. The girls walked
closer to the sound of the children's
voices.

"Yes, but I think someone's singing out
of tune!" Rachel whispered.

Kirsty nodded. She had noticed one
child who was a little
shorter than the
others. He was
wrapped up in a
big coat with
a hood, and a
long thick scarf.
He was singing
very loudly . . .
but not very well!

"It's the one in the
big coat," she whispered.

"He may not be able to sing very well," Rachel whispered back, "but he's got the best candle!"

Kirsty stared at the candle. It was bigger and rounder than the ones the other children were holding, and was a very pure white color. It almost seemed to glow with hidden fire! Looking closely, Kirsty saw tiny white and silver sparkles swirl around the candle.

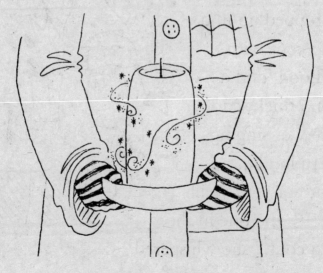

"Rachel, I think he has the magic candle!" Kirsty gasped. "He must be a goblin!"

Her heart thumping with excitement, Rachel stared at the caroler. As he moved, she caught a glimpse of a green nose poking over the top of his scarf.

"It *is* a goblin!" she said to Kirsty. "But how are we going to get the candle back from him?"

"Hello, Rachel!" a tiny voice sang out beside her.

Rachel jumped, and turned to see Stella peeking out from behind a shiny glass ball on the Christmas tree.

"I spotted my magic candle, too!"
Stella whispered, as Rachel and Kirsty
gathered around to hide her from sight.
"But I don't know how to get it back.
Any ideas?"

Rachel and Kirsty were silent for a
minute, thinking. Then Kirsty's face
broke into a smile. "I thought of
something that might work!" she said.
"Stella, could you use your magic to
make a copy of the magic candle?"

"Yes, I think so," Stella replied. "But it won't be magical, like the real candle."

"That doesn't matter," said Kirsty, "as long as it fools the goblin!"

"I'll do my best," Stella promised. She frowned in concentration and waved her wand. Immediately, green sparkles whizzed and fizzed around in front of her!

A Sweet Trick

The green sparkles faded away, and a candle appeared in Kirsty's hand. It was a perfect copy of the magic candle — except that it was pink!

"Whoops!" Stella laughed. "Let's try that again."

She waved her wand. This time, as the sparkles died away, Rachel and Kirsty watched the candle slowly turn from pink to white.

"Perfect!" said Kirsty, tucking the candle into her pocket. "Now, wait here." Kirsty headed across the square while Rachel and Stella kept an eye on the goblin. When she came back, she was carrying two paper bags.

"What's in there?" Rachel asked
curiously.

"Candy!" Kirsty replied, opening the
bags. Rachel peeked in and saw
striped mints in one bag and
fruity hard candies
in the other.

"Now, you take
these, Rachel,"
Kirsty said, handing
the mints to her friend as the
carolers finished their song. "Go
offer all the carolers a treat!"

Looking confused, Rachel did as she
was told. "Merry Christmas!" she said,
holding the bag out to the singers closest
to her.

"Oh, thank you!" they replied, each
taking a mint.

Kirsty watched the goblin as Rachel kept handing out candy. He was looking very eager as he waited his turn, but before Rachel reached him, Kirsty stepped forward. "Here, have some candy!" she said, holding out her bag.

Greedily, the goblin thrust his gloved hand into the bag and pulled out a whole fistful of candy. He didn't even say thank you! But a look of dismay

came over his face as he stared at the candy in his hand. Kirsty grinned. The goblin had just realized that he couldn't unwrap his candy and hold the candle at the same time!

Now Rachel and Stella could see what Kirsty's plan was!

"What's the matter?" Kirsty asked the goblin. "Don't you like candy?"

"Yes, but I can't unwrap these while I'm holding this candle!" the goblin grumbled.

Kirsty held out her hand. "Why don't you let me hold it for you?" she offered politely.

Rachel and Stella exchanged a hopeful look as they waited for the goblin to reply.

"Oh no!" the goblin said quickly, his eyes moving from side to side. "This is a very special candle."

"But I'll be standing right next to you the whole time," Kirsty assured him.

The goblin still looked doubtful, so Rachel decided to help Kirsty out. She took a piece of candy from Kirsty's bag and unwrapped it right under the goblin's nose. Then she popped it into her mouth.

"Mmm!" she said. "This candy is delicious!"

The goblin stared longingly at the candy while Kirsty held her breath. Would he give in and let her take the candle . . . or not?

Candlelight

After a moment, the goblin couldn't stand it any longer. "Here!" he said gruffly, thrusting the magic candle at Kirsty.

Kirsty took the candle and breathed a silent sigh of relief. Now that his hands were free, the goblin started unwrapping candy as fast as he could. Then he

crammed a whole handful of pieces into
his mouth at the same time.

While the goblin was stuffing himself,
Kirsty quietly pulled out the fake candle.
Quickly, she swapped the two candles,
slipping the magical one into her pocket.

"I'll take that back now," the goblin
mumbled through a mouthful of candy.
He snatched the candle from Kirsty and
turned his back on her.

Kirsty winked at Rachel. They moved
over to the Christmas tree
where Stella was hidden.

"Good work, girls!" the
little fairy
whispered, her
eyes shining. "You
have the candle!"

"And the goblin
hasn't even
noticed!" Kirsty
laughed.

They all looked over at the
goblin, who was happily trying to sing
through a mouthful of candy.

"Let's take the candle back to
Fairyland, where it belongs!" Stella said.
While everyone was watching the
carolers, she raised her wand and

showered Kirsty and Rachel with fairy
sparkles. The girls felt themselves
shrinking to fairy size as they were
whisked away in a swirl of magic dust.

A few moments later, the girls were
flying over Fairyland with glittering,
gauzy wings on their backs. Below, they
could see red and white toadstool houses.
The fairy palace was up ahead, with a
huge Christmas tree standing in front of it!

As Stella and the girls fluttered down to the ground, they saw the king and queen waiting to greet them.

"We have the magic candle!" Stella announced.

"Kirsty and Rachel, welcome to Fairyland once more!" said King Oberon.

"You have found our magic candle!" Queen Titania added happily. "We cannot thank you and Stella enough."

"We're glad to help," Kirsty said, and Rachel nodded.

Stella turned toward them. "Girls, would you like to put the candle back on the tree?" she asked.

Both girls nodded, and Kirsty took the candle from her pocket. The branches of the tree were decorated with candles in silver holders, but the biggest and most beautiful holder was empty.

As Rachel held the branch steady, Kirsty carefully slotted the candle into place. Immediately, it began to glow, giving off magical, fiery sparks. "We'll do our best to find the glass ball and the star, too," Rachel promised the king and queen.

"Thank you," said Queen Titania with a smile. "And now you must return to Wetherbury and see how beautiful it looks, now that you two brought the magic candle home!"

She lifted her wand. Rachel and Kirsty just had time to wave good-bye to Stella before they were whisked away in a swirl of silver sparkles.

A moment later, the girls found themselves back in Wetherbury square.

Nobody seemed to have noticed that they'd vanished and reappeared again!

Everyone was too busy staring up at the beautiful Christmas snowflakes, which were now shining brightly.

"Look, the goblin still hasn't realized that he's been tricked!" whispered Kirsty.

The girls glanced at the goblin, who was singing away happily. Then they joined the crowd of shoppers admiring the snowflakes. Every single bulb was now lit, and the glittering snowflakes stood out beautifully against the velvety night sky.

Kirsty beamed at Rachel. "Aren't they pretty?"

Rachel nodded. "It's a good start," she said. "Now we have to find the glass ball and the star."

"Yes," Kirsty agreed with a smile. "But right now, we'd better work on our Christmas shopping, or our  friends and families won't get any presents this year!"

"You're right!" Rachel laughed, and the two girls headed for the stores, with the snowflakes shining brightly overhead.

Snowballs and
Glass Balls

Contents

A Snowy Start

"Kirsty! Wake up!"

Kirsty rolled over in bed. "What's the matter, Rachel?" she asked sleepily.

Rachel, who was at the window in her pajamas, grinned at her. "It's snowing!"

"Really?" Fully awake now, Kirsty bounced out of bed and rushed over to the window. She peered outside. Flakes

of white snow were drifting down from
the gray sky.

"I hope it snows for days," Rachel said
eagerly. "It would be so cool to have a
white Christmas."

"Look, it's falling faster and faster,"
Kirsty pointed out.

The girls stood at the window for a few minutes, watching the snowflakes swirl, before they got dressed. The snow began to settle on the lawn and flowerbeds, and showed no signs of stopping.

"If we get a lot of snow, we could go to the park after lunch and build a snowman," Kirsty suggested, as she brushed her hair.

"Ooh, that sounds great!" Rachel exclaimed.

The girls went downstairs. In the living room, Kirsty's

dad was on his hands and knees tinkering with the Christmas tree lights. Mrs. Tate was helping him.

"Good morning, girls," she said with a smile. Mr. Tate scratched his head. "I don't understand it," he muttered. "We checked the wiring and the fuse is fine, but these lights still won't come on."

"Why don't you take a break and have some breakfast?" suggested Kirsty's mom.

"Not yet," Mr. Tate replied, frowning. "I think I've almost got it. . . ."

Smiling, Mrs. Tate shook her head and went to the kitchen. Rachel and Kirsty followed.

"The lights won't come back on until the magic glass ball has been returned to Fairyland," Kirsty whispered to Rachel. "Maybe we'll find it today."

After breakfast, the girls spent the morning wrapping Christmas presents. They kept an eye on the weather. To their delight, the snow fell heavily all morning, and by lunchtime the backyard was covered with a thick, white blanket of snow.

 After lunch, the girls slipped on their coats and boots. "Mom, can Rachel and I go to the park?" Kirsty asked. Mrs. Tate nodded.

"Make sure you're home in time for dinner. Hopefully, the lights will be fixed by then," she added with a smile, "otherwise I'll have to start serving your dad his meals under the tree!"

Rachel and Kirsty laughed, and rushed out the back door. They stomped through the snow in their boots, and by the time they got to the park their cheeks were pink and glowing.

The park was full of people. Some were building snowmen, others were sledding and having snowball fights. But Rachel and Kirsty quickly found a quiet spot, not far from a group of six children who were building a snowman.

"Let's make the snowman's body first,"
Kirsty suggested, rolling a snowball in her
mittened hands. She put it on the ground,
and she and Rachel began to roll it
around in the snow so it got bigger and
bigger. Then they made a smaller
snowball for the head.

"See if you can find some pebbles,
Rachel," Kirsty panted, as she lifted the
snowman's head onto the top of his body.

Rachel dug around in a flowerbed and managed to find a small handful of pebbles. She and Kirsty pressed the pebbles into the snowman, giving him eyes, a mouth, and four buttons down his chest.

"Isn't he handsome?" Kirsty said with a grin.

"Not without a nose!" Rachel laughed. "I'll look for a twig or something."

"Will this do?" called a tiny voice.

The girls spun around and stared up at the sky. Stella the Star Fairy was flying toward them, clutching a long, thin carrot in her arms!

"Perfect!" Kirsty agreed, as Stella landed on the snowman's head. She took the carrot and stuck it right in the middle of the snowman's face.

"What are you doing here, Stella?" asked Rachel.

"Do you think the glass ball might be nearby?" added Kirsty eagerly.

Stella nodded and flew over to sit on Rachel's shoulder. "Look over there," she whispered, pointing to the group of children nearby. "And take a good look at that snowman!"

A Very Suspicious Snowman

Wondering what Stella meant, Rachel and Kirsty glanced over at the group of children. They had finished their snowman and were now having a snowball fight. The girls edged closer to the other snowman, staring at it curiously.

It wasn't like any snowman they'd ever seen before. For a start, it looked *mean*! It

had a big nose made with a large,
pointed stone, a grinning mouth made of
black pebbles, and enormous feet
of snow.

"It looks like a snow goblin!" Kirsty
said slowly. Then she gasped and pointed
at the children. "And if that's a snow
goblin, who are they?"

"Maybe they're Jack Frost's goblins in
disguise!" Rachel whispered.

"Exactly!" Stella replied. "In which case, they might have the glass ball."

"I think we need to take a closer look," Kirsty said firmly.

Trying to keep out of sight, the girls made their way around the flowerbed and closer to the snowman. None of the children noticed them. They were too busy hurling snowballs at each other.

The girls peered at them, but they were so bundled up in hoods, scarves, and

coats that it was hard to tell if they were
goblins or not.

As the girls watched, one of the children
was hit in the face by a big snowball.
With a screech of rage, he tore off his
wet scarf, revealing a mean, green face!

"They *are* goblins!" Kirsty exclaimed.

"I'll get you for that!" the goblin yelled,
shaking the snow from his big nose and
stamping his foot. "I'm going to shove a
snowball down the back of your neck!"

"You'll have to catch me first!" the goblin who had thrown the snowball jeered. He kicked lumps of snow at the other goblin, then ran away to hide behind a tree, laughing his head off.

"The glass ball might be around here somewhere," Rachel said hopefully. "Maybe we should look for it."

"We'll have to get a bit closer," Kirsty said, creeping forward.

"Please be careful, girls," Stella whispered anxiously.

Rachel and Kirsty began to edge
toward the goblins. Stella sat on Rachel's
shoulder and peeked out from under her
hood. Snowballs were flying everywhere!
As Kirsty, Rachel, and Stella watched,
a goblin wearing a red scarf threw a
snowball so hard that he slipped and fell
on his face.

"Ha, ha, ha!" the other goblins roared
with delight.

Moaning and grumbling, the goblin scrambled to his feet. "Stop laughing at me!" he spluttered through a mouthful of snow. Then, as one of the laughing goblins bent to make another snowball, the goblin with the red scarf rushed over and shoved a snowball down the back of his blue coat.

"Arggh!" yelled the goblin in the blue coat. "That's cold!"

"They're so covered in snow, they look like snow goblins themselves!" Kirsty muttered, trying not to laugh. Rachel giggled, then covered her mouth with her hand. She didn't want the goblins to notice her!

Suddenly, Kirsty frowned. "What's that goblin doing over there?" she whispered.

Until now, neither Stella nor the girls had noticed that one goblin was sitting on the ground, cross-legged, rolling snowballs. He had obviously decided that the best way to win the fight was to gather lots of snowballs in advance. There was already a large pile of them

beside him! As he carefully rolled
another, a goblin in a green hat dashed
over and tried to take a snowball from
the top of the heap.

Looking furious, the sitting goblin
dropped the snowball he was holding,
and slapped the other's hand. "Make
your own snowballs!" he shouted, and
went back to rolling snowballs.

Kirsty looked at him a little more closely, and then nudged Rachel. "Look," she hissed.

Rachel saw that there was something round and sparkling in the goblin's lap, but it wasn't a snowball. It was pure

white, even whiter than the snow, and it flashed and glittered in the sunlight with every color of the rainbow.

"It's the magic glass ball!" Stella whispered in delight.

Girls Under Fire

"It's beautiful!" Rachel sighed. "We have to get it back."

"But how?" Kirsty murmured thoughtfully.

The girls and Stella watched the goblins, wondering how they could get ahold of the glass ball. The sitting goblin was much more interested in snowballs than the glass ball, but he kept glancing up suspiciously to check that none of the other goblins were trying to steal from his snowball pile. That made it tough for the girls to get close to him without being seen!

Meanwhile, the snowball fight was getting fiercer. The goblin in the blue coat had hurried off to hide behind a tree and shake the snow out of his clothes. But the one in the red scarf snuck around the other side of the tree, threw an armful of snow over his rival, and then ran off to hide behind two other goblins.

Yelling with rage, the goblin in the blue coat ran after him and flung a big snowball at his enemy. Unfortunately, it hit the two other goblins. They shrieked with fury.

Now almost all of the goblins were covered in snow and ready to fight!

They started taking sides — the goblin in the red scarf and his two friends, against the goblin in the blue coat and the one in the green hat.

"Hey!" the goblin in the red scarf shouted to the sitting goblin, as he and his teammate were pelted with snowballs. "Come and help us! It's two against three here!"

The sitting goblin grinned and jumped
to his feet. He didn't
realize that as he
did so, the glass
ball fell off his
lap and landed
softly on the
snowy
ground.
He quickly
scooped up
his snowballs
and ran to join the fight.

Rachel and Kirsty glanced at each
other.

"Let's try and grab the glass ball!"
Rachel whispered.

Kirsty nodded.

As the goblins hurled snowballs at each other, Kirsty and Rachel began to edge their way toward the glass ball. It lay there, sparkling prettily, but just as Kirsty was  about to stretch out her hand and pick it up, a large snowball suddenly hit her on the shoulder. "Stop them!" shouted a gruff goblin voice.

The girls had been spotted, and all six goblins were now running in their direction, flinging snowballs at them!

"Quick!" Rachel gasped, as a snowball hit her on the arm. "Behind that tree!"

Forced to leave the glass ball where it was, Rachel and Kirsty dashed behind the tree. A huge shower of snowballs followed them.

"How are we going to get the glass ball back now?" Rachel panted. "We can't get past six goblins!"

"Wait!" Stella said suddenly. She flew up to a branch of the tree, her eyes shining. "I'll turn you girls into fairies, and then we'll all be small enough to dodge the snowballs!" she declared happily.

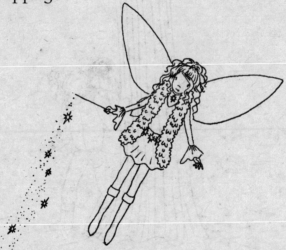

"But if the goblins are throwing snowballs at us, that means they know we're here," Kirsty pointed out. "And we don't want them to see us."

"Oh yes, we do!" laughed Stella. "We want the goblins to see us and pelt us with snowballs!"

Kirsty and Rachel stared at Stella, confused.

"How will it help to have lots of snowballs thrown at us?" asked Rachel.

"Trust me!" Stella told her with a grin. "My plan is going to work. I'm sure of it!"

A Daring Plan

Rachel and Kirsty had no idea what Stella was up to, but they both loved being fairy-size. They waited eagerly while Stella waved her wand and scattered magic fairy dust over them. A moment later, they had shrunk to the same size as their fairy friend. Magical fairy wings shimmered on their backs.

"Here we go!" Stella said, fluttering out from behind the tree. "Now make lots of noise, girls, and make sure the goblins see us!"

Still confused, Kirsty and Rachel zoomed up into the air behind Stella and headed toward the goblins.

"Yoo-hoo!" Rachel called, waving her arms.

"Over here!" yelled Kirsty.

While Stella and the girls had been behind the tree, the goblins had been stockpiling snowballs.

Now they looked up, and their
warty faces darkened with rage.
"Here come those pesky
fairies!" one goblin shouted.
"Get them!"
snarled another.
All of the goblins began
hurling snowballs at Rachel,
Kirsty, and Stella.
"This is scary!" Kirsty
panted as a large snowball
whistled past her ear.
Now that she was so
tiny, the snowballs
seemed as big as houses!
"Good job, girls!" Stella
called, as Rachel fluttered
out of the way of another
snowball. "Now, watch!"

As yet another snowball whizzed past Stella, she lifted her wand and sprinkled magic fairy dust over it. Rachel and Kirsty watched curiously as the snowball changed in midair to become an exact copy of the magic glass ball.

"Look!" shouted the goblin in the blue coat. "One of you just threw the glass ball instead of a snowball! What a fool!"

"Who're you calling a fool?" yelled the goblin with the hat, tossing a snowball at him instead of at Stella and the girls.

"Stop it!" the first goblin panted, dodging out of the way. "We have to get the glass ball back!"

Arguing and grumbling, the six goblins chased after the fake glass ball, which had fallen to the ground just below Rachel, Stella, and Kirsty.

"Keep those fairies away from the glass ball!" shouted one of the goblins. As they ran, the goblins all began hurling snowballs at Stella, Rachel, and Kirsty again.

"Can you see the real glass ball, girls?" called Stella.

Rachel and Kirsty peered through the storm of snowballs. The glass ball had rolled to a stop near the edge of the flowerbed.

"I see it!" Rachel shouted.

"Good," Stella replied, raising her wand again. "You go and get it while I give the goblins something else to chase!"

She waved her wand, and suddenly the air was full of magic sparkles. This time, to Kirsty and Rachel's amazement, all the snowballs flying through the air turned into glass balls!

"What's going on?" yelled the goblin in the red scarf, hardly

able to believe his eyes. He skidded to a
halt as the glass balls began to fall to the
ground around him. The other goblins
banged right into him. They all ended up
in a snowy heap!

"Pesky fairies! Which is the real glass
ball?" one goblin spluttered. They all
began to scramble around, picking up
the fake ones.

In the meantime, Kirsty and Rachel swooped down to the edge of the flowerbed.

"We'll both have to lift the glass ball, now that we're fairy-size," Kirsty said as she landed on the ground. "And we'll have to do it quickly, before the goblins see what we're up to!"

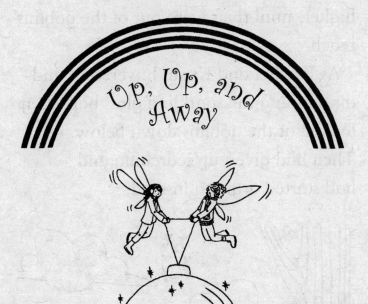

Up, Up, and Away

Rachel and Kirsty both grabbed onto the glass ball.

"Now!" Rachel whispered.

Both girls fluttered their wings, struggling to fly upward while lifting the glass ball. To their relief, it was just light enough for them to carry. Gradually, the girls rose into the air, higher and higher, until they were out of the goblins' reach.

As Rachel and Kirsty hovered in mid-air, holding the sparkling glass ball, they looked at the goblins down below. They had given up searching and had started arguing instead.

"Who threw the glass ball in the first place?" one of them grumbled.

"Well, it wasn't ME!" another goblin retorted.

"I bet it's YOUR fault!" the first goblin shouted, prodding another in the stomach.

"No, it's HIS fault!" that goblin snapped, pushing the goblin in the green hat over. With a howl of rage, the green hat-wearing goblin tumbled backward into a deep snowdrift and disappeared from sight.

Immediately, the other goblins began pushing and shoving each other until they all ended up stuck in the snowdrift, their arms and legs waving frantically.

Meanwhile, a beaming Stella flew over to join Rachel and Kirsty. "We did it, girls!" Stella cried, her eyes shining. "And now I think it's time to take the magic glass ball straight back to Fairyland."

She lifted her wand. In a whirl of green sparkles, Rachel and Kirsty were whisked away, the goblins' grumbles ringing in their ears.

As they flew over Fairyland, Rachel and Kirsty looked down to see a large crowd of fairies waiting around the Christmas tree by the royal palace. Everyone looked very anxious, but when they saw Stella, Rachel, and Kirsty flying toward them with the glass ball, they clapped their hands in joy.

"Thank you, thank you," cried Queen Titania, coming to greet the girls as they landed.

"Our glass ball ornament is safely home again," King Oberon declared, smiling.

"Rachel, Kirsty, would you put it back on the tree for us?" Stella asked sweetly.

"We'd love to!" Rachel and Kirsty chorused. They carried the glass ball over to the tree.

There were ornaments on every branch, except for a big one near the middle. Carefully, the girls hung the glass ball on the branch. It swayed gently, glittering and gleaming and sending flashes of rainbow colors here and there.

"We left the goblins stuck in a snowdrift!" Stella told the king and queen with a grin.

"They were arguing so much, it'll take them ages to dig themselves out!" Kirsty added.

Everyone laughed, but then Queen Titania sighed.

"Stella, Rachel, and Kirsty," she said solemnly, "you have done very well to return the candle and the glass ball. But the last decoration, the star, is the most important one of all!"

"Why?" Rachel asked.

"Because without the magic star, the stars will not twinkle in the night sky," the queen explained. "And without the stars, Santa Claus can't find his way to deliver the presents on Christmas Eve."

"You mean nobody will get any presents?" Kristy gasped.

The queen nodded sadly.

"And Christmas Eve is tomorrow," Rachel said. "We don't have much time left!"

"At least we know where the star is," Stella pointed out. "It's hidden somewhere in Goblin Grotto."

"Then we'll have to go there and get it back!" Kirsty said in a determined voice. "Can you take us, Stella?"

The little fairy nodded solemnly.

"We won't let you down," Rachel told the king and queen firmly.

"Thank you," Queen Titania replied. "And now I

111

think you both deserve a good rest. Go home, and forget all about the goblins until tomorrow."

The two girls said their good-byes as the Fairy Queen waved her wand. In a swirl of fairy dust, the girls were swept up and carried home. They landed gently on Kirsty's front doorstep.

"We have to find the star tomorrow, Kirsty," Rachel said.

"Yes," Kirsty agreed. "Christmas just won't be Christmas without Santa!"

Suddenly, Rachel pointed at the living room window. "Look, Kirsty!" she said, smiling widely. "Your Christmas tree lights are working again!"

"Hooray!" Kirsty cried happily.

The two girls rushed inside.

Mr. Tate was sitting on the couch, looking very pleased with himself. "Well, I fixed the lights, girls," he announced. "It was just a matter of changing every bulb on the string."

Rachel and Kirsty smiled at each other.

"That's what Dad thinks," Kirsty whispered.

"But we know better!" Rachel added.

Search for
the Star

Contents

Girls Become Goblins!

"I wonder what Goblin Grotto is like," Rachel said, excitedly. It was Christmas Eve, and she and Kirsty were out in the Tates' backyard, sweeping the snow off the paths. "Do you think it'll be scary?"

"I hope not!" Kirsty replied with a laugh, brushing away the last heap of snow.

"But don't forget, we'll have Stella
there with all her fairy magic to help us!"

Rachel grinned and nodded. "But how
will we get the star without the goblins
seeing us?" she went on. "I mean, even if
we're fairy-size, there's still a chance
we'll be spotted."

"I know," Kirsty agreed. "But it's not
going to stop us from trying, is it?"

"Of course not!" Rachel said in a determined voice. "We have to get the star back, or there will be no real stars in the sky to guide Santa when he's delivering presents!" Then she shaded her eyes and gazed across the yard. "Kirsty, look at that cute little robin."

Kirsty looked where Rachel was pointing. A robin was bobbing through the air, coming straight toward them.

"There's something on its back," Kirsty said in surprise.

"Hello, girls!" called a tiny voice.

"Stella!" Rachel gasped.

The fairy was riding along on the robin's back, waving at Rachel and Kirsty. The little bird landed on the fence. Stella hopped off and patted the robin's head. It flew away into a nearby tree.

"Are you here to take us to Goblin Grotto?" asked Rachel.

Stella nodded. "Are you sure you want to do this, girls?" she asked, her face very serious.

"Of course we do!" Rachel replied firmly.

"But we're worried about being spotted by the goblins," Kirsty added. "We need some sort of disguise."

"Oh!" Rachel exclaimed suddenly. "Maybe we could disguise ourselves as *goblins*!"

"That's a great idea!" Kirsty agreed. "Could you make us goblin-size and green, Stella?"

"Oh yes!" The fairy laughed.

"If we wrap scarves around our faces and put up our hoods like the goblins have

123

been doing, no one will even notice us!"
Rachel said happily.

"Here goes!" Stella cried. She waved
her wand, sending sparkling fairy dust
spinning all around the girls.
Immediately, they shrank down to the
size of goblins.

"Am I green?" asked Kirsty. Then she

caught sight of
Rachel's face
and burst out
laughing. Her
friend was as
green as the
greenest goblin!
Rachel was
laughing too
hard at Kirsty's
face to answer.

"You're both green all over!" Stella said with a smile, as the girls took off their gloves and laughed again at their green fingers. "There's just one problem, though," the fairy went on with a frown. "My magic can't make you look mean and nasty like the goblins. So you'll have to do that yourselves."

Kirsty and Rachel were still giggling at each other's faces.

"Try to look as angry and grumpy as you can," Stella told them.

Rachel and Kirsty managed to stop laughing. Rachel screwed up her face into a frown, while Kirsty scowled and narrowed her eyes.

"That's not mean and nasty enough,"
Stella declared. "Try again!"

This time, both girls hunched their
shoulders and screwed up their faces into
the ugliest, grumpiest frowns they could
manage.

"Well, you don't look *quite* as nasty as
real goblins," Stella said, laughing, "but
it'll have to do."

"Let's wrap ourselves up, Rachel," Kirsty said. "That will help hide our faces."

Quickly, the girls wound their scarves around the lower part of their faces, and pulled up their hoods.

"Now," Stella went on, "are you ready to come with me to Goblin Grotto, my goblin friends?"

Both girls nodded eagerly. With a flick of Stella's wand and a shower of magic sparkles, they were on their way!

Starshine in Goblin Grotto

Seconds later, in a whirl of fairy magic,
Stella, Rachel, and Kirsty arrived at
Goblin Grotto. The two girls had never
been there before, and they stared
around curiously.

The goblins lived in small wooden huts
that were dotted around the foot of a
snow-covered hill. Smoke curled from

the chimneys of all the houses. The
ground was covered with thick snow and
ice, and the sky overhead was grim
and gray with no sign of the sun. At the
top of the hill, Rachel and Kirsty could
see Jack Frost's ice castle. A cold, gray
mist drifted around its frozen blue turrets.

"*Brrr*," whispered Kirsty, wrapping her arms around herself. "It's even colder here than it is at home!"

Rachel, who was closest to one of the wooden huts, peered cautiously through the window. A fire was burning merrily in the fireplace, and a goblin was slumped in an armchair in front of it. He was stretching out his toes near the flames and mumbling under his breath.

"Oh, my feet are frozen!" he complained.

Rachel smiled. "Look," she whispered to Kirsty. "I'd forgotten how much goblins hate to have cold feet."

Kirsty peeked through the window and grinned.

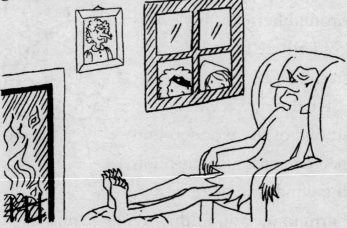

"Girls!" Stella gasped, tapping Rachel on the shoulder. "Someone's coming!"

Suddenly feeling very scared, Rachel and Kirsty spun around. A big goblin with a wart on the end of his nose was tramping down the snowy path toward them.

"Quick, Stella!" Kirsty said urgently. "Hide!"

"All right," Stella whispered. "But put on your grumpiest faces, girls."

The fairy fluttered out of sight behind the wooden hut, and Kirsty and Rachel screwed their faces up into ugly frowns. Hearts thumping, they waited as the goblin came closer. Would he realize that they were humans in disguise, and not goblins at all?

As the goblin passed, he threw the two girls a grumpy look. "What are you staring at?" he snapped.

Rachel and Kirsty didn't reply, and the goblin trudged on his way. Both girls sighed with relief.

"Our disguise worked!" Kirsty said.

"Well done, girls," Stella said, flying out from behind the hut. "Now we must find the star!"

Rachel's face fell. "But how are we going to do that?" she asked. "We can't search the houses if there are goblins inside them."

Kirsty nodded thoughtfully and gazed around. Suddenly, her eyes opened wide. "Actually, I don't think *finding* the star is going to be a problem," she said. "But getting it down might be!"

Rachel and Stella looked confused.

"What do you mean, Kirsty?" asked Rachel.

"Look," Kirsty replied, pointing down the path.

Stella and Rachel turned to see what Kirsty was pointing at.

There, in the middle of the goblin village, above the roofs of the wooden huts, they could just see the tip of a tall Christmas tree. Perched on the very top was a large, silver star. It shimmered and shone in the cold, gray air. And as it sparkled, every so often it sent dazzling

darts of silver fairy dust shooting into the sky.

"It's the star from the Fairyland Christmas tree!" Stella exclaimed in delight. "You found it!"

Catch a Falling Star

Rachel, Kirsty, and Stella stared up at the star.

"Quick, let's go and get it right away!" Stella whispered urgently.

As fast as they could, the girls hurried along the snow-covered path to the center of the village.

"How will we get the star down?" Kirsty asked anxiously.

"Without all those goblins seeing us!" Rachel added, stopping dead as she stared at the scene ahead of her.

A crowd of grown-up goblins and goblin children were gathered near the Christmas tree, having a party. They were all wrapped up in hats, scarves, and coats. One was selling food, and there was a group of carolers holding lanterns. They were all singing out of tune, just like the goblin who'd had the magic candle. They sounded so bad that Kirsty wanted to put her hands over her ears! "Goblins aren't very good singers, are they?" she whispered to Rachel. Rachel shook her head. "But they seem to be enjoying themselves," she whispered back, as the goblins launched into another tuneless song. "We have to get the star down somehow," Stella said thoughtfully.

"Girls, if I fly up and push the star off the top of the tree without being spotted, can you try to catch it?"

"Yes, that's a great idea!" Rachel said with a grin.

"We'll go and stand under the tree, as close as we can get," Kirsty whispered to Stella. "Good luck!"

Stella zoomed off, and Rachel turned to Kirsty.

"Let's join the party," she said. "But we'd better try and sing out of tune, or they might guess that we're not real goblins!"

Putting on their nastiest faces, Rachel and Kirsty hurried over to join the carolers. None of the goblins gave them a second glance as they stood at the back of the group. Then the girls began to sing, doing their best to sound flat and tuneless as they inched closer to the tree.

"There's Stella!" Kirsty whispered to Rachel.

Rachel glanced up. Stella was flying high overhead, taking cover behind the gray clouds. She hovered above the tree, looking around nervously, and then began to float downward.

Suddenly, the goblin standing next to Kirsty elbowed her in the ribs. Kirsty almost fell over with fright. Had he

noticed Stella? "You're singing out of tune!" he said with a scowl. "Sorry!" Kirsty muttered, as gruffly as she could. She decided to sing more quietly.

Rachel could see that Stella had landed on the top of the tree, and was now releasing the star from the cords that held it in place. When she was ready, the little fairy waved at Rachel. Carefully, Rachel edged up next to the tree. As Stella pushed the star gently off the top, Rachel held out her hands.

The star fell toward her, sparkling as it tumbled through the air. It seemed very bright to Rachel. She was sure one of the goblins would spot it! But, to her relief, nobody seemed to notice, and she caught it safely before it hit the ground. Quickly, she tucked it inside her coat, and edged her way back to Kirsty.

"I've got it!" she whispered joyfully.

"Great!" Kirsty beamed.

"What are you whispering about?" snapped the grumpy goblin next to her. He stared curiously at the girls, and they both began to feel nervous!

"Do your best grumpy face," Rachel muttered.

She and Kirsty pulled their faces into angry frowns, but the goblin didn't stop staring.

"Look!" one of the other carolers

shouted suddenly. "The star is missing from the top of the Christmas tree!"

All the goblins looked up, and began to mutter angrily as they saw that the star had disappeared.

"Where is it?"

"Did it fall off?"

"Who took it?"

Then there was another shout from the goblin selling food. "Look up there!" he cried, pointing toward the top of the tree. "Is that a *fairy*?"

Run Away!

Rachel and Kirsty stared at each other in horror, then glanced up at Stella. The tiny fairy must have heard the goblin's cry, because she darted quickly out of sight behind one of the large glass balls hanging on the tree.

Rachel looked down at the front of her coat. To her dismay, she saw that magical, silvery sparks were shooting out from between the buttons. "Oh no!" she whispered.

The goblin next to Rachel noticed the sparks, too. He was staring at them! He peered at Rachel's face, and he suddenly frowned. "You're not a goblin!" he hissed, stepping in front of her. "You've stolen our star!"

Just then, Kirsty, who was still staring up at the tree, felt her hood slip backwards.

"A girl!" yelled the goblin standing next to her. He was staring at Kirsty as if his eyes were going to pop out of his head. "A human girl!"

"And they've got the star!" screeched the goblin who had spotted Rachel.

Rachel pushed past him and grabbed Kirsty's hand. "RUN!" she yelled.

The two girls broke away from the crowd of goblins, but the goblins ran after them, shouting and pushing each other out of the way. Kirsty looked back at the tree anxiously and saw Stella zooming after them.

"Which way?" Rachel panted, as they came to a fork in the path.

"This way!" Kirsty took off down the left-hand fork, and Rachel followed. She glanced back over her shoulder, and her heart sank. Other goblins were coming out of their houses to see what was going on, and they were joining in the chase. Now there were about fifty goblins running after the girls!

"What's going on?" shouted a gruff voice ahead of them. Rachel and Kirsty saw the goblin who had been warming his toes by the fire, standing in the middle of the path. Like the other goblins, he had heard the noise and had come outside to see what was going on.

"Stop them!" shouted the goblins

behind the girls. "They've stolen the magic star!" The goblin held up his hand. "STOP!" he roared. But Rachel and Kirsty didn't stop. They dashed past the goblin, one on either side of him. The goblin was spun around like a top. He

landed on his
back in the
snow.

"Oh!" he
howled. "I'm
frozen!"

"Come on, girls!" Stella urged. She
had caught up with Rachel and Kirsty,
and now she hovered over their heads as
they ran down another path.

Kirsty was trying desperately to think of an escape plan. *If Stella turns us into fairies, we can fly away!* she thought, but then she realized that it wouldn't work. The star was too big for a fairy to carry, and they couldn't leave it behind.

Suddenly, she noticed that they were running back into the middle of the village. Both girls skidded to a stop by the Christmas tree.

"We ran around in a great big circle!" Rachel groaned.

"And here come the goblins!" Kirsty panted, her face pale.

The goblins were rushing toward them from all directions.

"Now we've got you!" one yelled, and the others cheered.

Kirsty turned to Stella. "Stella, if Rachel and I were fairy-size, do you think the three of us could carry the star together?" she asked urgently. "Each of us could hold a corner of it."

"I don't know," Stella replied doubtfully. "It's awfully heavy."

"We'll have to try!" Rachel gasped, laying the star carefully on the ground. "It's our only chance!"

As the goblins surrounded them, Stella raised her wand.

"There's the star!" one of the goblins shouted. "Grab it!"

But before the goblins could move, Stella's magic fairy dust drifted over Rachel and Kirsty. Immediately, the goblin green faded away and the girls shrank down to fairy-size. Both girls couldn't help shivering with fright as they gazed around at the angry goblins, getting closer and closer. They looked much bigger and scarier from a fairy's point of view!

"Quick!" Kirsty shouted, as the circle of goblins began to close in on them. "Grab a corner of the star and fly up — as fast as you can!"

Flight to Fairyland

A moment later, Rachel, Kirsty, and Stella shot up into the sky, lifting the star with them.

"We did it!" Rachel cried joyfully.

The goblins couldn't believe their eyes. They were so surprised, they couldn't stop themselves from colliding with the Christmas tree — and each other — as they rushed forward. They all bumped their knobby knees and long noses, and fell into a tangled heap on the ground, groaning loudly.

"Watch out for the Christmas tree!" one of them shouted.

Hovering high above the ground, Stella, Rachel, and Kirsty watched as the huge Christmas tree tottered and swayed from side to side. Slowly, it toppled over.

There were shrieks of rage as some of the big goblins were covered with tree branches, tinsel, and other decorations. A group of goblin children who were watching laughed so hard that *they* fell over, too! Stella turned to Rachel and Kirsty, a big smile on her face. "Let's get back to Fairyland right away!" she said. "It's almost dark, and

Santa will want to start delivering his presents soon!"

Carrying the star, Stella, Rachel, and Kirsty flew to Fairyland as fast as their wings would take them. When they arrived, they found every single fairy in the land waiting for them around the Christmas tree, along with King Oberon and Queen Titania. All the fairies gasped with delight as they spotted Stella and the girls flying toward them with the magic star.

"The star!" the fairies shouted excitedly. "Christmas is saved!"

"You're just in time," King Oberon declared, beaming at Stella, Rachel, and Kirsty as they landed clutching the star. "Santa Claus is about to set off!"

"Thank you so much," added Queen Titania gratefully. "Now, would you put the star back on the tree where it belongs?"

Stella, Rachel, and Kirsty flew to the top of the tree and carefully lowered the star into place.

The star immediately shot dazzling swirls of magical silver fairy dust from every point, as if it knew it was home again.

"Girls, we all thank you from the bottom of our hearts!" the king declared, as Rachel and Kirsty flew down to stand before him. "We can never repay you fully, but we can promise you an extra-special Christmas!"

All of the fairies laughed and clapped, and Kirsty and Rachel looked at each other in delight.

"Thank you for your help, girls," Stella said, kissing them both lightly on the cheek. "I hope you get everything you want for Christmas!"

"Now, we mustn't keep you any longer," the queen added. "You have to be home in time to enjoy your own Christmas, after working so hard."

"Merry Christmas, everybody!" Kirsty and Rachel called, as Stella lifted her wand to send them home.

"Merry Christmas!" the fairies replied.
They all waved their wands in farewell.
Kirsty and Rachel were swept gently off
their feet in a whirl of sparkling magic.

As the mist of fairy dust faded away,
the girls found themselves back in Kirsty's
snowy backyard. It was getting dark,
and the lights were on in the Tates'
house.

"Look!" Rachel pointed up at the sky. "The stars are out!"

Kirsty glanced up and saw that the stars were twinkling brightly, like tiny diamonds. "What's that over there?" she asked, pointing at a large shape moving swiftly across the sky.

Rachel squinted and tried to make out

what the shape could be. "It looks like
a . . . sleigh," she said slowly.

Kirsty's eyes opened wide. "It's Santa
Claus!" she gasped.

The two girls watched in wonder as
Santa's sleigh, pulled by his magic
reindeer, zoomed across the sky, leaving
a trail of golden sparks behind it.

"Oh!" Kirsty cried suddenly. "The
sparks behind the sleigh spell out a
message!"

Rachel caught her breath, her heart pounding with excitement. She and Kirsty stared up at the dark sky. There, against the inky blackness, they could clearly read the words, 'Merry Christmas, Rachel and Kirsty!' written in dazzling golden sparks.

As he passed over the Tates' house, Santa Claus looked down and gave the girls a friendly wave, grinning cheerfully at them. Then the sleigh picked up speed and disappeared behind a cloud.

"He waved to us!" Kirsty laughed.

"That was amazing!" Rachel agreed, her eyes shining as she watched the golden letters fade away into the darkness.

"Girls!" Mrs. Tate called from inside the house. "Rachel's parents are here to pick her up."

"I think it's going to be a very merry Christmas, Rachel," Kirsty said with a

grin, as she and Rachel ran toward the house.

"Yes. Merry Christmas, Kirsty!" laughed Rachel. "And a merry Christmas to everyone in Fairyland!"

RAINBOW magic™

THE PETAL FAIRIES

Coming soon!

Here's a sneak peek at the first book,

Tia the Tulip Fairy!

A Fairy Garden

"I think the Fairy Garden must be through here," Rachel Walker said, pointing to a wrought iron gate. She and her friend, Kirsty Tate, were exploring the grounds of Blossom Hall, an old hotel where their families were staying over spring break. Both girls had been interested to hear the owner of Blossom

Hall, Mrs. Forrest, mention the Fairy Garden. After all, Kirsty and Rachel knew a lot about fairies: they were friends with them!

"It's known as the Fairy Garden because there is a perfect ring of tulips growing in the middle of it," Mrs. Forrest had explained. "We call it the Blossom Fairy Ring."

As soon as they'd finished their breakfast, Rachel and Kirsty had asked their parents if it was all right for them to go exploring. They were eager to look around during the sunny morning. From what they could see through the windows, the gardens were very pretty, with their pink and white flowering cherry trees, long rolling lawns, and masses of cheerful flowers.

"Of course you can explore," Mr. Tate had said. "Just make sure you stay inside the grounds of Blossom Hall."

Now Rachel eagerly lifted the latch of the gate. "Here we are!" she said, pushing it open.

The girls stepped into the walled garden together. "It's beautiful!" Kirsty exclaimed, taking in the rambling roses that climbed the walls and the old stone fountain in one corner.

"It's the kind of place you can imagine a real fairy visiting," Rachel said, smiling. "And that must be the Blossom Fairy Ring!" she added, pointing to a circle of yellow and orange tulips.

"How pretty!" Kirsty said, going over for a closer look. She noticed that some of the tulips were wilting. But then she stopped and listened carefully. "Rachel, can you hear someone crying?" she asked in a whisper.

Rachel stood still, listening hard, then nodded. "I can't see anyone else here, though," she whispered, gazing around. "Who could it be?"

The girls looked around the small garden, but it wasn't big enough to have many hiding places. The crying was definitely louder near the fairy ring. It seemed to be coming from the tulips!

Kirsty looked inside the nearest tulip — and gasped. Sitting at the bottom of the flower, with her face in her hands, was a tiny fairy!

Fairyland is never far away!
Look for these other

books:

The Rainbow Fairies

#1: Ruby the Red Fairy

#2: Amber the Orange Fairy

#3: Sunny the Yellow Fairy

#4: Fern the Green Fairy

#5: Sky the Blue Fairy

#6: Inky the Indigo Fairy

#7: Heather the Violet Fairy

The Weather Fairies

#1: Crystal the Snow Fairy

#2: Abigail the Breeze Fairy

#3: Pearl the Cloud Fairy

#4: Goldie the Sunshine Fairy

#5: Evie the Mist Fairy

#6: Storm the Lightning Fairy

#7: Hayley the Rain Fairy

The Jewel Fairies

#1: India the Moonstone Fairy

#2: Scarlett the Garnet Fairy

#3: Emily the Emerald Fairy

#4: Chloe the Topaz Fairy

#5: Amy the Amethyst Fairy

#6: Sophie the Sapphire Fairy

#7: Lucy the Diamond Fairy

The Pet Fairies

#1: Katie the Kitten Fairy

#2: Bella the Bunny Fairy

#3: Georgia the Guinea Pig Fairy

#4: Lauren the Puppy Fairy

#5: Harriet the Hamster Fairy
#6: Molly the Goldfish Fairy
#7: Penny the Pony Fairy

The Fun Day Fairies
#1: Megan the Monday Fairy
#2: Tara the Tuesday Fairy
#3: Willow the Wednesday Fairy
#4: Thea the Thursday Fairy
#5: Felicity the Friday Fairy
#6: Sienna the Saturday Fairy
#7: Sarah the Sunday Fairy

Special Editions
Joy the Summer Vacation Fairy
Holly the Christmas Fairy
Kylie the Carnival Fairy
Stella the Star Fairy
Fairy Friends Sticker Book
Fairy Fashion Dress-Up Book
Rainbow Magic Door Hanger Book

And coming soon, The Petal Fairies!